For my family

and my son Michael, who
inspired me to write
this book, and for all the
children who feel different
or have food allergies.

www.mascotbooks.com

Bittersweet Holidays

For more information, please contact:
Mascot Books
560 Herndon Parkway #120
Herndon, VA 20170
info@mascotbooks.com

Library of Congress Control Number: 2017911972

CPSIA Code: PRT0817A
ISBN-13: 978-1-68401-381-4

Printed in the United States

This book is not intended as a substitute for the medical advice of physicians. The reader should regularly consult a physician in matters relating to his/her health and particularly with respect to any symptoms that may require diagnosis or medical attention.

BITTERSWEET
Holidays

Written by *Nadya Klimenko*

Illustrated by *Rayanne Vieira*

It was a beautiful autumn day and a little bear named Misha was getting ready for school. However, he was not a regular bear. You see, he has food allergies.

The school had been decorated for fall when he arrived. All the festivities, celebrations, parties, cookies, candy, and thoughts of trick-or-treating should have made him excited, but instead he just felt a little sad and worried.

In his classroom, everyone was busy making invitations and decorations for their class party. Misha, however, didn't feel like joining in and sat alone at the back of the classroom.

"What's wrong?" asked Cody the Labrador puppy. "Come join us!"

"I would," Misha said, "but Halloween and other holidays aren't much fun for me. I have food allergies, so I can't eat any of my trick-or-treating candy or holiday party cookies."

"Food allergies?" Cody asked. "That sounds serious! What are those?"

Misha's teacher Ms. Right overheard and came over to the group. "Food allergies are very serious!" she said. "It means that Misha is very sensitive to some food. Even the smell of specific food can make him dangerously sick."

"Yes, I'm allergic to peanuts, tree nuts, and coconuts, even though coconuts aren't really nuts. I am also allergic to other foods."

"So you can't have a peanut butter and jelly sandwich?" asked Crunchy the chipmunk. "I love PB&J!"

"No, I can't. I might be ok with eating a jelly sandwich, but not one with peanut butter," Misha replied. "Also, sometimes foods come in contact with others at the factory and can contain traces of nuts or other things I'm allergic to, so I need to be very careful and always read the food labels!"

"That must be so hard!" said Lola the kitten. "Is that why you sit at a separate table at lunch time? My cousin is allergic to milk and dairy. She can't have ice cream!"

"I'm allergic to dust mites and get very itchy around carpets," Cody said. "I also have seasonal allergies to pollen and sneeze during spring time."

"Yes, allergies aren't fun," Misha said. "I am sorry to hear that you also have uncomfortable allergies, Cody! As for me, I feel left out at holiday

parties because I can't eat the same cookies or candy as everyone else. Sometimes even the smell of fish, eggs, or peanuts can make me sick and make bumps pop up on my skin."

"What else can happen?" Cody asked.

"Sometimes I get this itchy feeling in my nose, then a runny nose. Sometimes I sneeze very quickly. Sometimes my throat feels itchy, and then it becomes so tight I have trouble breathing. I have to know these signals my body sends so I can recognize them and get help in time. I always need a good emergency plan."

"You see," Ms. Right said, "food allergies are no joking matter. Someone with food allergies can get very sick from eating, touching, or even just smelling certain foods. That's why it's very important for us to know if one of our friends has food allergies. This way we can be careful about what we eat or drink around them. We also need to wash our hands carefully, as food can be on our hands and can transfer to other things we touch."

"I'm glad you shared with us!" Cody said. "Now I'll know to hide foods you are allergic to when you come over to visit my house. I don't want you to be sick! Also, I will ask my mom to make an allergy-free cake for my birthday so we can all share it and be safe! A party is much more fun when friends are there! I don't want you to be left out!"

ALLERGY FREE
ZONE

"My doctor said there are 8 major allergens," Misha said. The most common are milk; eggs; peanuts; tree nuts such as almonds, cashews, and walnuts; fish; shellfish like crab, lobster, and shrimp; soy; and wheat. There are others such as sesame seeds and corn."

"Let's look around and see if we can make the room safe by finding all the possible allergens hiding in the room!" Ms. Right said.

"We always want to include all our friends in our holiday fun! What holidays does everyone celebrate?"

"LABOR DAY!"

"Halloween!"

"Thanksgiving!"

"Look at each other," said Ms. Right. "Each of us is unique and different in our own ways. We have different eyes and different fur. Some of us speak different languages and have different cultures and traditions. Yet we all share this classroom, read the same books, and learn the same things. So we need to share our time together kindly and safely. We need to understand and respect each other, not make fun of our differences. Friends like to help their friends, right?"

"Right! We are different in our own ways, and we even celebrate different holidays!" the kids shouted out.

"Let's do this," said Ms. Right. "If you have any allergies, or any other special dietary restrictions, please ask your parents to list them and bring the list to school with you next week. We'll make sure that our holiday parties and our classroom are safe and fun for everyone!"

"Thank you, Ms. Right," said Misha. "Holidays are hard for me because everyone has treats, candy, and things I'm afraid to come into contact with or eat. There are desserts and fun parties with food and sweets, but for me holidays can be bittersweet.

Sometimes I feel very sad and lonely, especially when people offer me candy that I am allergic to. My allergies mean I have to miss out on fun activities. It would be so nice if we could share things that aren't food. Why does it always have to be candy?

"You're right, Misha!" Ms. Right responded. "What else can we make or give as gifts?"

"Pretty pencils!"

"Stickers!"

"Books!"

"Glow sticks!"

"A soccer ball!"

"Art supplies or drawing materials!"

"Blocks and toy characters!"

"Handmade gifts or cards!"

Next week, Misha's class had the best party ever. There were allergy-safe treats that considered the traditions of others, along with healthy treats like fruits and vegetables to make kids strong and healthy! All the kids brought gifts other than candy to exchange too!

But most importantly, everyone thought about each other and their unique and different needs. After all, we share the same space every day. We share our classrooms, our time, and our planet. We can all make a difference by being kind and caring to each other. "Thank you for making this a safe holiday with good friends and fun," Misha said. "Have a *Safetastic* holiday season, everyone!"

WHAT IS A FOOD ALLERGY?

ACCORDING TO THE MAYO CLINIC, "a food allergy is an immune system reaction that occurs soon after eating a certain food. Even a tiny amount of the allergy-causing food can trigger signs and symptoms such as digestive problems, hives, or swollen airways. In some people, a food allergy can cause severe symptoms or even a life-threatening reaction known as anaphylaxis."

ACCORDING TO FOODALLERGIES.ORG, approximately 1 out of 13 children has food allergies. This is almost two children in every classroom, so chances are someone in your classroom has food allergies. Wouldn't it be nice to help your classmates be safe?

Misha says: Always be careful with new foods! It is best to avoid the food that you are allergic to. When someone offers you a new food, you can politely say, "No, thank you!" Walk away if someone continues to offer or push you to eat this food. Ask for help if needed, and learn to read food labels.

HOW DO WE FIND OUT ABOUT ALLERGIES?

Misha says: Doctors have special tests to diagnose food allergies. These tests can range from skin scratch tests to more serious ones like a blood test. Although these can be a little uncomfortable, they are very important to help keep us safe. And you can get stickers or something else for being brave! A doctor will provide you and your family with a plan and explain how to manage your allergies.

When someone eats a new food, they can have a reaction to it. Their stomach can hurt, their skin can begin to itch, they can begin sneezing, have a runny nose, watery eyes, or have swollen lips and puffy eyes. They also can develop bumps called hives on their skin. Other symptoms of an allergic reaction can include an itchy feeling and tightness in the throat, which can lead to breathing difficulties. If this happens, serious medical help is needed.

Misha says: Make a plan for an emergency that is your unique plan. Tell your family, friends, and teachers about your allergies. Also, if you have a friend with allergies, help them recognize these signals and get help by calling a parent, a teacher, or a school nurse. Always have your emergency medication with you! Ask your friends not to share new food with you and learn to read the labels! Avoid taking new foods from anyone. Be careful and safe!

HAVE A SAFETASTIC HOLIDAY SEASON!

For more information about food allergies, diagnoses, treatments, and education, go to **foodallergy.org.** A portion of the proceeds from this book will be donated to FARE (Food Allergy Research and Education) to help support food allergy research, awareness, and education.

Activity: Can you find the peanuts and other allergens hiding around the pages of the book? We want to make sure our school and classrooms are safe and allergy free.

(Answer: 13 peanuts, 1 basket of eggs, and 1 fish)

A LIST OF THE TOP 8 ALLERGENS

Peanuts

Tree nuts
(almonds, cashews, walnuts, & others)

Milk

Eggs

Fish

Shellfish
(crab, lobster, & shrimp)

Soy

Wheat

There are other allergens as well, such as sesame seeds and corn.

About the author

Nadya Klimenko, PsyD holds a doctoral degree in Clinical Psychology and has been working in the field of mental health for many years. Dr. Klimenko specializes in working with children and educating families about the importance of healthy lifestyles and healthy nutrition. She is also passionate about raising awareness of food allergies and other unique special needs children and families encounter every day. She resides in Virginia with her family.